INTRODUCTION FOR PARENTS

S*ammy the Elephant and Mr. Camel* is a delightful and profound story that can be enjoyed by children of all ages. Although the story was originally created for a boy who was a bed wetter, we have found that its theme of a struggling youngster who is guided to discover his own unique abilities can touch the heart of any child in a universal way.

When we presented *Sammy the Elephant and Mr. Camel* to our young client, we offered it simply as an enjoyable story. He was never told that the story had anything to do with his bedwetting problem. On a conscious level, the little boy delighted in the storyline of Sammy, a lovable little elephant who kept spilling his buckets of water. At the same time, on an unconscious level, he was being given a comprehensive healing metaphor – a symbolic story – that mirrored his own failure and frustrations in attempting to gain control over his bedwetting.

As the story unfolds, Sammy the Elephant, together with our young listener, is re-introduced to his own inner strengths and abilities through the guidance of Mr. Camel. After Sammy goes through a learning period during which he has the pleasures of discovering how many things he can do well, there is a crisis – a fire near the circus – and a resolution, as Sammy saves the day. He has, indeed, learned many new things with the help of Mr. Camel. Sammy emerges from his experiences with a new sense of self-appreciation. Children reading the story, or having it read to them, will also learn new ways to feel better about themselves as they travel with Sammy and Mr. Camel.

You may read *Sammy the Elephant and Mr. Camel* to your child simply as an entertaining story. Or, if you choose, you may read it slowly, emphasizing the words in italics by making your voice softer or deeper. This subtle shift in your voice helps to activate your child's inner strengths and abilities in a special way. The beauty of this kind of storytelling is that it enables children to apply the many lessons interwoven throughout the story to other areas of their lives where issues of control and self-appreciation are important.

Perhaps as you read this story to your child, you too may notice the many discoveries made available to you in delightful and surprising ways from your own child within.

JOYCE C. MILLS, PH.D., AND RICHARD J. CROWLEY, PH.D.

The circus is coming to town!

Imagine the excitement! Hear the shouting and the stomping as the big tent goes up, UP, UP. The tent is so big it *can easily hold everything within.* Imagine all of the acrobats, the jugglers, the tightrope walkers, the trapeze artists, the dancers, and the clowns.

Did you know that everyone helps put the circus together?
The acrobats hook up the high wires.
The clowns hang the flags.

And the strong animals
carry big buckets of water
and the heavy beams
that hold up the circus tent.

The elephants are the strongest of all. They move the beams
and water buckets by carrying them with their trunks.
Imagine a big, strong elephant carrying a big, heavy beam.
Hear the sound he makes. Watch him wrap his trunk around
it. See how easily he carries it!

At the circus all of the elephants were
doing their work very well. All except
for one small elephant named Sammy.

Sammy wrapped his trunk around the handle of
a large bucket of water, like all the other elephants.
He began to lift it and *hold it*, but soon…BOOM!
The bucket fell to the ground. Imagine the sound as
the bucket landed. Imagine seeing it begin to roll.

Sammy hoped that nobody noticed. But they did.

"What did you do that for?" yelled Carla.

"It almost rolled over my paw!" roared Fritz.

"Can't you *hold on to it longer,* the way everyone else does?" bellowed Harriet. She was the oldest elephant.

Sammy got scared.

Sammy decided that maybe he hadn't paid enough attention.
So he watched the other elephants carry water and heavy beams.
He watched them very closely, then tried again.

Sammy wrapped his trunk around the handle of the bucket.
Then *using all those muscles,* he easily picked up the bucket.

Sammy *felt so good inside* as he walked along, swaying from side
to side, bringing the bucket to where it was needed.

But suddenly…BOOM! Down again! This time the bucket rolled so far that it knocked over all the other buckets. Water spilled everywhere. Everyone was angry with Sammy.

"Can't *you control that* bucket yet?" yelled Jeremiah.

"*You can hold that water,*" said Phillipa. "All the elephants do. They *hold it very well*. Just watch what they do to carry the water."

Well, by now Sammy was quite frustrated. Imagine how he felt. He tried and tried, day after day, but…BOOM! Down went the buckets of water every time. Sammy felt that everyone in the circus was upset with him and gave him mean looks. Sammy did not know how to please them. He felt ashamed of himself and sad.

"I am trying, but no one understands," he cried. "No one really cares."

One day when Sammy was feeling very sad,
Mr. Camel heard him sniffling.

"You don't look very happy, Sammy," he said.
"Is there anything I can do to help you feel better?"

"I don't know," Sammy answered. "I keep trying
to *hold on to that* bucket, to do my part.
But I keep spilling it. I keep letting it go too soon."

Mr. Camel thought for a moment.
Then he began reminding Sammy of all the things
that Sammy had learned to do.

"When you were born," said Mr. Camel, "you couldn't walk right away. There was a time when your legs were shaky. *You had to learn* to take each step, one after the other. At first you had a hard time, but *you continued to practice and to learn.* After a while, you learned to walk successfully."

"You also learned how to pick up grass with your trunk and eat it,"
Mr. Camel reminded Sammy. "*You learned* how to eat all by yourself.
Now your trunk can carry just the right amount of food to satisfy you.
You learned to know when you are full and comfortable, when you feel
good inside. You may be surprised to realize how long *you can hold
on to that good feeling. Now you can hold on to that good feeling for a long,
long time,* Sammy."

Sammy thought for a few minutes and then answered,
"Yes, I remember that. I can do that."

"It's just like Bonnie the Bicyclist," said Mr. Camel.
"I remember when she couldn't even ride a bicycle.
She would get up on her bike and fall down. As a matter of fact,
someone had to teach Bonnie how to *hold on* to the handlebars
correctly. She had to practice for a long time. After she *learned to
hold on*, she was finally able to *relax and enjoy the feeling of letting go.*"

"When you watch her, Sammy," Mr. Camel advised,
"pay attention to that look on her face and notice the fun
she is having *being in control* of her bicycle."

"This reminds me of Jingles the Juggler, too," said Mr. Camel. "I remember when Jingles first came to the circus. All he could juggle were two little bowling pins."

"Now he can juggle balls and large bowling pins and dishes. He can juggle everything together at the same time. His balance is perfect. He *knows exactly when to hold on and when to let go* of each of those things."

"You just have to *trust you can do it*. Some things take a little more time to learn than others, Sammy. And you have time to *learn that now*."

Suddenly Sammy and Mr. Camel heard sirens.
They looked up and saw flames in the distance.

"There's a fire at that farmhouse!"
Mr. Camel cried.
"But the fire engine can't get there.
The bridge is washed out!
The only way to put out that fire is for
elephants to carry water in their
trunks and spray it on the fire.
But the other elephants are way
across town practicing
for the opening day parade."

Sammy looked at Mr. Camel.
"What can we do?" he asked.

"It's up to you now," Mr. Camel replied.

"What do you mean?" asked Sammy.

"I'm going to teach you something important," said Mr. Camel. "Listen very closely. As you know, camels *carry water for a long, long time.* I'm going to teach you how to do that, so *you can carry water for a long time,* too. And once *you can learn to do that,* you will be able to go over to the lake, put your trunk in, hear the water going into your trunk, and *hold on to it for a long time. You will be able to hold on to it successfully.*"

"Then you will see yourself walking over to where the fire is and putting out the fire by *letting go of the water at just the right time and in just the right place.* Not a hundred feet before, not ten feet before, not even one foot before – but only when you are exactly at the right spot. Then you will aim your trunk and let go of the water."

"Just remember a time when you held on to a special, happy feeling for a long time," said Mr. Camel. "Maybe you carried the excitement for a long time, wondering what gifts you would be getting on your birthday. Everyone knows elephants have good memories and always remember everything that is important. *Remember something you learned a long time ago and still carry happily with you now.*"

"After listening to you, Mr. Camel," said Sammy, "I can see myself doing all of that. I feel I can do it now."

So Mr. Camel and Sammy went over to the lake, and Sammy took in as much water as he could hold comfortably. Then Sammy began the long walk over to the fire. And Sammy got all the way there. Just as Mr. Camel had told him, Sammy let go of all the water at exactly the right time and place. The sound of that water hitting the fire at the right time gave him such a happy, joyful feeling inside. Sammy used his new ability again and again until the fire was completely out.

Soon everyone arrived at the farmhouse.
Sammy heard everyone clapping and cheering.
His face lit up. He felt good inside.

"Hurray, Sammy!" they all shouted.
"You did it!"

Sammy felt special for the first time in a very long time.
He knew he now had a *special ability* —
being able to hold on to the water for a long time
and knowing exactly when and where to let it all go.

As the days went by, Sammy was *able to discover*
other abilities that he had forgotten about. He thought,
"Once you know how to hold on to the water,
you can hold on to anything." At that moment,
Mr. Camel came walking by.

Sammy saw him and shouted, "Watch this, Mr. Camel!" He picked up a heavy wooden beam. He brought the beam all the way over to the center of the tent where it belonged. As he gently set it down, Sammy felt wonderful inside. Imagine him letting go of the beam so securely and hearing it land so gently.

Mr. Camel smiled at Sammy and said,
"*You have learned that and much,
much more.* You are an important part
of the circus, and *you will continue
to learn more and more each day.*"

Weeks later, after the tent was up, Sammy saw Mr. Camel again while he was practicing a balancing trick. He wanted to join the acrobat act when he got bigger.

Mr. Camel reminded Sammy, *"Any time you want to see yourself doing anything in the future, just remember all the important things you've already learned. You can learn anything else you need, just by taking your time and holding on to those happy memories."*

Sammy nodded his head.
"Thank you, Mr. Camel,"
he said, "for reminding me of
something I knew all along."

NOTE TO PARENTS
by Jane Annunziata, Psy.D.

In this story, Sammy struggles with a common childhood problem. The medical term for this problem is *enuresis,* which refers to the child's difficulty urinating at the appropriate time and place. This problem is generally something children cannot control, and it tends to be more common in children with family members who have (or had) enuresis. A child is never diagnosed with enuresis before age five. Enuresis can occur during the day (diurnal enuresis) or during the night while the child is sleeping (nocturnal enuresis).

Diurnal enuresis, or daytime wetting, is often associated with the child ignoring bodily cues and postponing going to the toilet because he is too busy with play or school activities. Most children who occasionally wet themselves during the day are able to outgrow this problem and learn to respond more promptly to their body signals to urinate. However, more persistent daytime wetting as the child gets older can be associated with emotional and behavioral problems and should be carefully watched.

Nocturnal enuresis, generally called bedwetting, is the most common type of enuresis and seems to occur more often in very sound sleepers. Sometimes the bedwetting occurs while children are dreaming, and they may recall a dream that involved urinating. Like daytime wetting, bedwetting is a cause for concern when it is frequent and beyond the age when nighttime dryness is expected developmentally.

Enuresis is diagnosed by a professional when specific criteria and behaviors are present. The diagnostic criteria for enuresis are:

🐘 The child must be at least five years old, or if developmentally delayed, the child must have a mental age of at least five years.

🐘 Wetting is not due to a medical condition or a medication the child is taking.

🐘 Wetting must occur at least two times per week and continue for at least three months. OR

🐘 The child must be experiencing very significant distress or impairment in a key area of life (e.g., at school or with peers) due to the wetting.

Many young children have bouts of wetting themselves before they gain full control of their bladders. As with learning any new skill, mistakes are inevitable, but most children do fully master the developmental milestone of toilet training by the age of five. Here are a few practical tips that can facilitate children remaining dry during the day and at night:

🐘 Rule out a physical cause for wetting with your child's pediatrician (e.g., urinary tract infection or other medical problem).

- Limit fluids after dinnertime. If the child is thirsty, offer ice cubes.
- Cheerfully and empathically remind children of the need to use the toilet during the day. For example, you might say, "I can see you're having so much fun with your toy cars, and I am sorry to interrupt you, but it's been a long time since you've been to the bathroom and I want you to stay dry and comfortable. I think it's time for a bathroom break. Your toys will wait for you."
- Give your children an age-appropriate amount of control over as many things as you can. For example, let them pick out which socks to wear or the color of their milk cup. Be especially mindful of control over toileting. For example, let them pick out a potty or ask them which bathroom they'd like to use.
- Talk with your child about any issues that might be stressing her or creating anxiety. If there is an obvious stressor in the family, speak to that and reassure the child about how you as a family will cope and help her. Additionally encourage your child to express feelings outwardly through drawing or playing rather than keeping them inside where they can cause anxiety.
- Stay positive and supportive about your child's wetting problem. Remind him of other problems that felt daunting that together you found a way to master.
- Modulate your own frustration. Parental outbursts of anger, while understandable, will only increase the child's anxiety and may worsen the problem.
- Use stories, imagery, and books to directly and indirectly address the underlying issues involved in mastering toilet training.
- Look for ways to highlight the areas where your child is competent, capable, and in control, and transfer that competence to master the current problem. For example, you might say to her, "You're so good at waiting your turn when you're in school. I bet you can practice doing the same thing here at home and wait until you get to the bathroom to urinate."

Sometimes a child has difficulty becoming fully toilet trained even after parents have tried many practical solutions and a physical problem has been ruled out. If problems with wetting continue and the child is beyond the age of five, it is best to consult a professional. Children can suffer a loss of self-esteem and meet with peer ridicule and rejection when they are not continent, especially once they enter kindergarten. Your child's pediatrician is always a good place to start. The pediatrician may suggest medication or a referral to a mental health professional. A mental health professional can evaluate your child to determine if there is an emotional component to the problem and may suggest any of the following (alone or in combination): parent guidance sessions (to help parents learn additional ways to work with your child), individual child therapy (play therapy), behavior modification, or family therapy.

Although enuresis can be a challenging problem to solve, remember that much help is available and that all children do learn to master this skill. As parents, you will feel pleased and proud once your child has mastered toilet training. And your child will feel so capable and in control (just like Sammy!) when this issue is resolved.

Jane Annunziata, Psy.D., is a clinical psychologist with a private practice for children and families in McLean, Virginia. She is also the author of many books and articles addressing the concerns of children and their parents.

ABOUT THE AUTHORS

JOYCE C. MILLS, Ph.D., is a Licensed Marriage and Family Therapist, Registered Play Therapy Supervisor, and recipient of the 1997 Play Therapy International award. Author of several books for all ages, she specializes in storytelling as a healing process. Dr. Mills is in private practice in Arizona and on the Board of Directors of the Turtle Island Project, where she co-leads healing retreats for women along with Native American spiritual and educational leaders.

RICHARD J. CROWLEY, Ph.D., has worked in the field of human behavior for more than thirty-five years. As a consultant to professional athletes, Wall Street traders, and corporate executives, his mental mechanics approach has gained international attention helping clients overcome their struggles and enhance their careers.

ABOUT THE ILLUSTRATOR

MARCY RAMSEY grew up in a big family in Connecticut. Her mother was an artist who gave her six children art supplies in order to keep them occupied while she painted, and so from an early age, Marcy has scribbled, dripped, and drawn her way through life. She has illustrated more than 50 books and written stories of her own.